CARELESS AT THE CARNIVAL
• JUNIOR DISCOVERS SPENDING •

BY DAVE RAMSEY
ILLUSTRATED BY MARSHALL RAMSEY

COLLECT ALL SIX ADVENTURES AT DAVERAMSEY.COM!

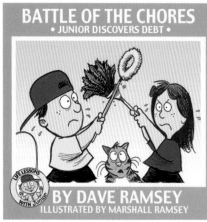

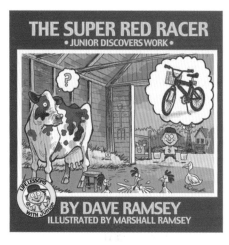

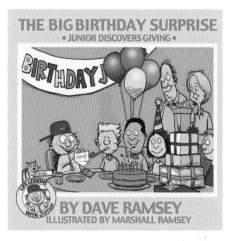

More fun than a barrel of money!

Dedication

Rachel is my middle child, the one who learned these principles as we lived them!
She has been our barometer to make sure we're teaching the kids well.
And in fact, she was the inspiration for this story!

Thank you, Rachel, for being wide-eyed and desiring to experience
life to the fullest while continuing to gain wisdom from your mom and dad.

www.daveramsey.com

 The children's group of Lampo Press

Careless at the Carnival: Junior Discovers Spending
Copyright © 2003 by Lampo Group, Inc.

Requests for information should be addressed to:
Lampo Press: 1749 Mallory Lane Suite #100 Brentwood, Tennessee 37027

ISBN 978-0-9726323-1-7

Second Edition

Written by: Dave Ramsey
Editors: Charlene Kever, Debbie LoCurto, LeeAnne Blair, Amber Kever
Cover Design and Art Direction: Marshall Ramsey

Printed and bound in The United States of America.

For more information on Dave Ramsey, go to: www.daveramsey.com or call (888) 227-3223
For more information on Marshall Ramsey, go to: www.clarionledger.com/ramsey

The Carnival. THE CARNIVAL! Junior loves the carnival. Every year his family goes over to the next county to THE CARNIVAL.

Junior rides EVERY ride. He especially loves the Tilt-O-Whirl because you go round and round and round, really, REALLY fast until your eyes bulge from your head! And, of course, Junior LOVES the Ferris Wheel. At the very top he can see ALL over the county!

And TODAY is THE DAY. This year, Junior is taking two friends, Billy Hampton and Esther Jones. Billy is Junior's best friend. They do everything together – eat, play ball, go to school and, yes, watch Dollar Bill's Adventures! Junior likes to hang out with Esther because she is smart and can run as fast as a boy!

Junior heard the doorbell and ran down the stairs to the front door. He opened it wide and said, "Hi, Billy." Billy and Junior did their top secret handshake.

"Hi, Junior" said Billy. "Are you ready to go to THE CARNIVAL?"

"I can't wait," said Junior. "We're going to have so much fun!"

Then, the doorbell rang again. Junior opened the door. "Hey, Esther."

"Hey, Junior. Ready to go?" asked Esther.

"SURE," replied Junior.

Junior yelled up the stairs, "Mom, Dad, everyone's here. Can we go to THE CARNIVAL now?"

Dad came down the stairs and let out the command, "Everyone in the van." They all ran and took their places and were off to THE CARNIVAL.

It wasn't long before they could see the Ferris Wheel high up in the sky. Esther yelled out, "We're almost there! I can't wait to ride the Ferris Wheel!"

"Me, too!" shouted Junior. "And eat a corn dog and cotton candy!" That made Mom's ears perk up and she gave them the "rules" for the day.

"Now, Junior. It will be important that you, Billy and Esther stay together at ALL times. Keep your money in your front pocket. And, by all means, children, don't spend ALL of your money on those silly carnival games. Very few people win the BIG prize and normally they pay a lot more for the prize than if they buy it at a store."

Billy said, "You are so right, Mrs. J., you can waste a lot of money on those silly games. I divided my money into envelopes. I have some for rides, some for food and some for playing a few games . . . that way I have money to do everything!"

"That's a great idea. Did you learn that on Dollar Bill's Adventures?"

Billy smiled and said, "Yes, Ma'am."

"Okay, team, we're here," said Dad. "Junior, you and your friends need to be back at this front gate no later than 4:30 p.m."

Billy, Esther and Junior all yelled out, "We'll see you then!" And they ran inside the gate.

"WOW," said Billy. "I can't believe all the rides. Okay, today it's MY turn to lead the way."

"You always lead," said Junior.

"Yes," said Billy, "and today it's very important because I know all about THE CARNIVAL and I have a map...so, off to the Tilt-O-Whirl!"

"Off to the Tilt-O-Whirl," Junior repeated. And all three began to run.

They passed by the corn dogs, the cotton candy and the funnel cakes, too. Junior felt his tummy getting ready for the yummy carnival food.

Then . . . there was GAMELAND.

"Look," Billy exclaimed, "The Balloon Race!"

The game man barked into his microphone, "Step right up, folks. Every game has a winner . . . first person to burst their balloon!"

"Let's play. I know one of us will win. We did bring GAME money," said Esther.

"Okay, let's play," said Junior.

They all sat down on a stool and pulled out a one dollar bill. Of course, Billy pulled his dollar from his GAME envelope.

The game man picked up their money and reminded everyone of the rules. "At the sound of the bell, shoot the water into the clown's mouth. That will fill up the balloon. The first balloon to pop will be the winner. Everyone ready?"

Junior, Billy and Esther all cheered, "READY!"

Junior closed one eye so he could aim better. The bell rang and they all began shooting water into the clown's mouth.

Junior could see his balloon filling with water, but so were Esther's and Billy's. The balloons got bigger and bigger and BIGGER until . . . POP!

Billy jumped up and down and twisted around. "I won! I won! I'm the winner!" he shouted.

"Yes, young man, you're the winner," announced the game man.

"I want the BIG blue teddy bear," said Billy.

"I'm sorry, son, you can only choose from the small prizes. The SUPER-DUPER-BIG prizes are for the winner when every seat is taken," explained the game man.

"Oh, well," said Billy. "I'll take the little duck key chain."

Billy put the key chain around his belt loop, shook his hips around and yelled, "I'm the winner!" Esther and Junior laughed and cheered.

"Look, Skee Ball! We can all play, put our tickets together and get a Really, Really, BIG prize," said Junior.

"Good idea!" agreed Esther. They each pulled out three dollars and exchanged them for tokens to play Skee Ball. Billy didn't have very much left in his GAME envelope.

They all began to play. Junior rolled his Skee ball straight up the middle, Billy did a fancy bank shot off the side, and Esther pulled her arm way back and let it go! Tickets were streaming out!

When they ran out of tokens, they counted their tickets . . . over 100! "That will get us a BIG Prize," said Billy.

They walked over to the counter to select a BIG prize. There was a CD player, a basketball and a remote-controlled car. But they didn't have enough tickets for any of the BIG Prizes, or even the medium-sized prizes, so they divided out their tickets. Billy got two more duck key chains, which he immediately attached to his belt loop. Esther got a pink, plastic ring, and Junior got a loopy-loop straw to use later in his thick chocolate milkshake.

"So much for games, let's go to the rides," said Esther, and she took off running. Billy and Junior ran after her.

All of a sudden, Esther stopped. She stopped so quickly that Billy and Junior bumped into her. Right there, in front of them, was a HUGE Dalmatian Dog.

Esther exclaimed, "That is the most beautiful Dalmatian Dog I've ever seen!"

He had black spots and a huge red bow. "Look at this great prize! And look, that man just won, so it can't be too hard. Let's win one!" she exclaimed.

Billy pulled out his GAME envelope. "Nope, not me, I've spent all my GAME money," said Billy.

Junior chimed in, "Me, too. I only have RIDE and FOOD money left."

"Come on guys, I know one of us can win," pleaded Esther with a sweet, sheepish smile.

"Ok," said Junior, "maybe just one game."

So, they all ran over to the dart game. The game man behind the counter was shouting out, "Three darts for a dollar! Three darts for a dollar!"

Esther ran up to the counter and laid down a crisp dollar bill. "Well, hello there, little lady. Are you ready to play the Dart Game?" asked the game man.

"Yes, Sir," said Esther. "I want to win the Dalmatian Dog!"

"Then step right up. For the BIG Prize, you have to burst all three balloons." Esther looked back at Junior and Billy. "I'm going to win that dog. Watch this." Esther pulled her arm back, set her feet, wiggled her hips, and sent the dart sailing through the air. POP went the balloon. "One down," she said.

She pulled her arm back again and threw her dart. POP went the balloon. "Good job, little lady," said the game man.

"Only one more and I get the Dalmatian Dog," said Esther. Junior and Billy began to cheer, "Go, Esther! Go, Esther!"

She picked up the last dart, took a deep breath, pulled her arm back, let the dart fly through the air and . . . BONK. The dart hit the board and bounced to the ground.

"You know, little lady, with an arm like yours, you might want to try again. I'm sure you'll win next time," said the game man.

So, Esther pulled another dollar from her pocket. She threw the first dart...POP, the second dart...POP, and the third dart...BONK. She missed!

"Come on, guys, let's all play. I just have to get that Dog!"

"Okay, Esther," said Billy. "We'll give it a try. But this is supposed to be my FOOD money."

All three stood at the dart line. Billy covered one eye and threw the dart. Junior pulled his arm straight back and threw the dart hard. No one could get all three balloons to pop. They all tried and tried and soon ALL of their FOOD money was gone.

UGH

POP

POP

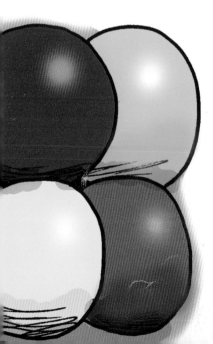

Then Esther started using her RIDE money. "Oh, please. I need this Dog. He will look so good in my room. Please help me get it."

Billy said, "Esther, Dollar Bill says it's like throwing your money away. You can go buy the Dog at the store for less money."

She stuck her bottom lip out and began to pout, "But I have never seen such a beautiful Dalmatian Dog anywhere. I need him!"

Billy and Junior pulled out their RIDE money and played and played and played… dollar after dollar after dollar.

The game man took Junior's last dollar and gave him three darts. Junior concentrated so hard. He aimed just right. POP went the first balloon, POP went the second balloon.

"Come on, Junior. I know you can win the Dog for me!"said Esther.

Junior took a deep breath. He rolled the dart in his fingers. He closed one eye and aimed for the balloon right in the middle of the board. He sent the dart sailing and . . . BONK.

"Hey, I'm sorry, kid. Better luck next time," said the game man.

The three friends left Gameland. ALL they had to show for ALL the money was a few duck key chains, a pink ring and a loopy-loop straw.

As they passed the food court, Junior was very sad. He felt his lower lip sticking out. "We don't have any money left for food. No corn dogs, no cotton candy, no thick chocolate milkshake," said Junior.

Then they saw the Tilt-O-Whirl. "Oh, no!" thought Junior, "I don't have money to buy a ticket for my favorite ride!"

He heard the loud music and saw all the other kids riding. They were laughing and yelling, with their eyes bulging out at each turn and twirl.

Billy pulled out all his envelopes and said, "I can't believe we used all of our money on the games. I had my money all divided into envelopes. Dollar Bill would be disappointed."

"Yes, and my Mom will be, too. We were CARELESS at the CARNIVAL spending all of our money on those silly games."

The three turned and pouted as they walked to the front gate to meet Junior's parents.

"Hello, children. Did you have a fun day at THE CARNIVAL?"

"Mom, we wasted all our money on games. We didn't get corn dogs, cotton candy, or a ride on the Tilt-O-Whirl," said Junior.

"Oh, Junior, I thought you knew better," said Mom.

"Yes, Ma'am. We did know better," said Billy.

"I wanted that big Dalmatian Dog so much," said Esther, "but we just threw our money away!"

"Well, children, I think you learned a valuable lesson about life today. You'll be happier if you make a plan for how you want to spend your money and then stick to the plan. You had enough money to play games, ride the Tilt-O-Whirl and Ferris Wheel, and eat…if only you would have followed your plan."

The next week Junior and his Dad got up early to go bargain shopping at yard sales. They always find great deals on things that people don't want anymore.

At their third stop, Junior couldn't believe his eyes. Back in a large box in the corner was a big Dalmatian Dog with black spots and a big red bow!

Junior ran and pulled the dog out of the large box. It was marked 50 cents. Junior reached into his YARD SALE envelope, pulled out two shiny quarters and made the biggest bargain purchase ever.

On the way home, Junior's Dad took him to Esther's house. Junior rang the doorbell. He held the Dalmatian Dog high over his head.

Esther opened the door and yelled with excitement, "Oh, Junior! Thank you! How . . . ? You didn't go back to THE CARNIVAL and waste more money, did you?"

"No," smiled Junior, "I learned my lesson about spending. I found this at a yard sale today for 50 cents, and bought it with my YARD SALE money!" They both laughed.

"Dollar Bill would be so proud," said Esther.

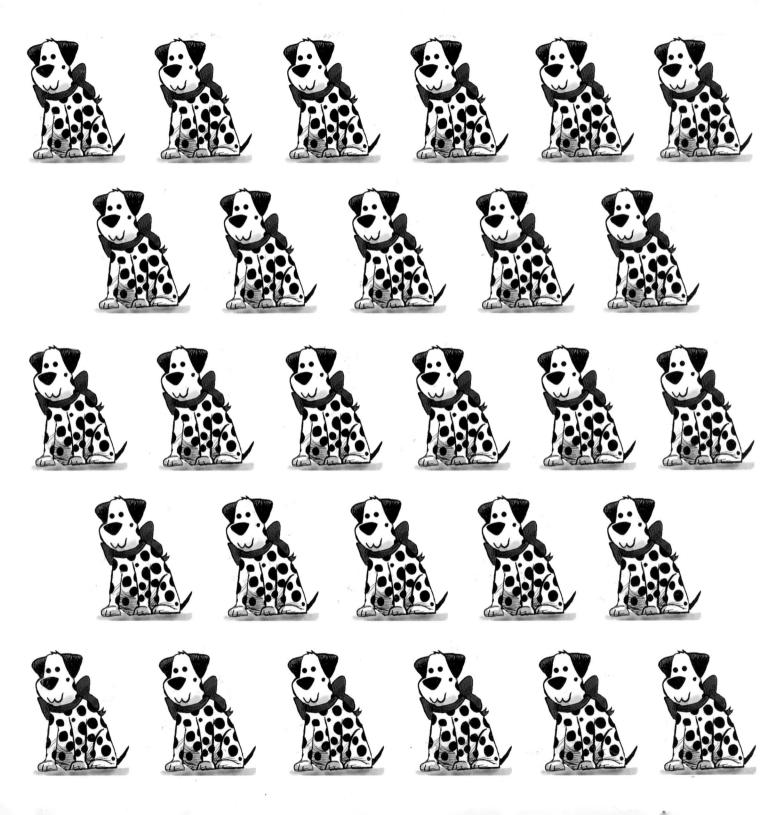